The Dragon's Revenge

CHARMSEEKERS: BOOK THREE

The Dragon's Revenge

Georgie Adams

Illustrated by Gwen Millward

Orion
Children's Books

First published in Great Britain in 2008
by Orion Children's Books
Reissued 2011 by Orion Children's Books
a division of the Orion Publishing Group Ltd
Orion House
5 Upper St Martin's Lane
London WC2H 9EA
An Hachette Livre UK Company

1 3 5 7 9 8 6 4 2

Text copyright © Georgie Adams 2008
Illustrations copyright © Gwen Millward 2008

The right of Georgie Adams and Gwen Millward to be
identified as the author and illustrator of this work
has been asserted.

A catalogue record for this book
is available from the British Library.

ISBN 978 1 4440 0291 1

Printed and bound in the UK by CPI Mackays, Chatham ME5 8TD

For Tom, with love.
A.T.

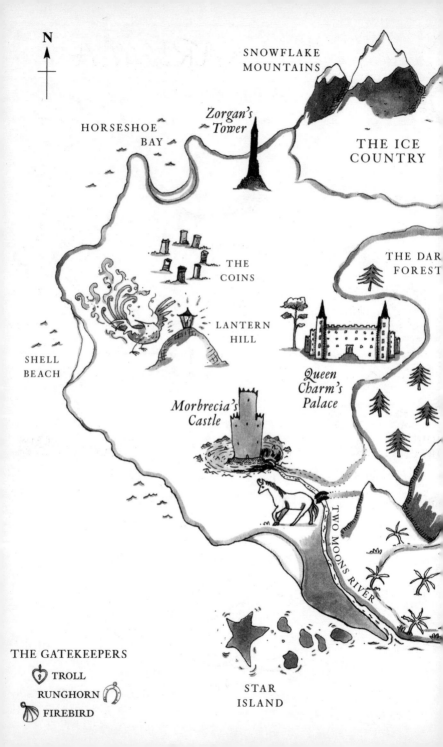

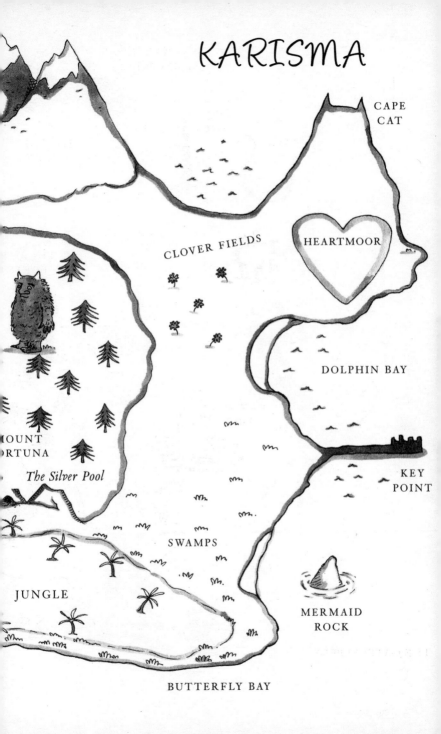

The Thirteen Charms of Karisma

When Charm became queen of Karisma, the wise and beautiful Silversmith made her a precious gift. It was a bracelet. On it were fastened thirteen silver amulets, which the Silversmith called "charms", in honour of the new queen.

It was part of Karisma law. Whenever there was a new ruler the Silversmith made a special gift, to help them care for the world they had inherited. And this time it was a bracelet. She told Queen Charm it was magical because the charms held the power to control the forces of nature and keep everything in balance. She must take the greatest care of them. As long as she, and she alone, had possession of the charms all would be well.

And so it was, until the bracelet was stolen by a spider, and fell into the hands of Zorgan, the magician. Then there was chaos!

Alone in her workshop, the Silversmith pauses in her delicate work to look upon the thirteen magic candles. Two have gone out. Eleven remain lit, each one a beacon of hope for its charm, yet to be found.

Will her Charmseeker return, to continue her quest? The Silversmith smiles as she resumes her work. Sesame Brown will be back, of that she is quite sure!

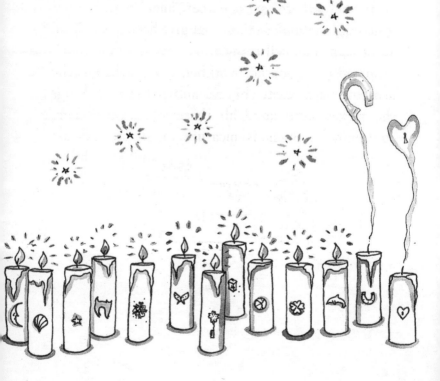

One

The Silversmith's workshop lies at the foot of Mount Fortuna, not far from the Silver Pool. Inside is a wonderful collection of curious objects, carvings, sculptures and ornaments that fire her imagination for her own beautiful creations. It is here she once cast the magical charm bracelet! And everywhere there is the sweet smell of mystica* from fragrant tinder-sticks that give her workshop an air of calm and well-being.

Spread neatly on her workbench are the tools she uses to shape, cast, engrave and polish the things she makes. And amid all these sits a small cup, containing a precious measure of silver, the last

* *

Mystica – an aromatic plant, native to Karisma. The petals produce a sweet smell when burned

drops she saved from the Silver Pool.

For many long days the Silversmith has been busy making a new crown. She works with infinite care and skill, hoping there will be just enough silver to finish it. She vividly recalls every moment of her mission to rescue what little remained of the Silver Pool. It happened not long ago . . .

5

On that particular day I had taken Queen Charm
to the Silver Pool. We had both been horrified to
see how quickly
the pool
was losing
silver. After
Queen Charm
had gone, I
returned and,
summoning
all my
courage, I
called
upon the
spirit of Agapogo.
All at once a wind
blew up and the force of it knocked
me back. Then the ghostly vision of
Agapogo appeared and looked so
angry that at first I was afraid.

6

But I spoke softly to Agapogo to calm her unhappy spirit.

"You have every reason to be angry," I said. "Zorgan has used his magic powers selfishly. You have been cursed to drain this precious pool for one purpose. So he can take his revenge on me!"

At the mention of Zorgan's name, Agapogo snorted and the air was filled with scalding steam.

"Zorgan is guilty of recklessly wasting the silver. But I must confess that I, and probably countless Silversmiths before me, have drawn silver from this pool without thinking it would ever run out. We've taken it for granted. We've always assumed the magical pool would refill, no matter how much silver was used. So we have been foolish too, Agapogo.

However, if you allow me one last measure of silver I will make amends, I promise. And you will be honoured throughout Karisma."

Agapogo's massive form glowed eerily and at last I heard her spirit sigh, as if some heavy burden had been lifted from her.

"Oh, Silversmith, good Silversmith,
Your words of wisdom ease my pain.
Your skillful craft has always been
In honour of our noble queen.
May your promise break this curse,
And Zorgan's evil plan reverse!"

Then Agapogo disappeared and I was left marvelling at the dragon's words. Taking a ladle, I scooped up the last drops of silver, poured them into a cup and took it safely back to my workshop . . .

Now the Silversmith twists the last few filigree strands of her design, turning it round and round to inspect her new creation.

"There is still one drop of silver left," she declares.

It was all part of her plan. And, if it worked, all would be well.

"The Crown of Agapogo!" exclaimed Queen Charm, examining every exquisite detail of the silver circlet. "Oh, it's beautiful! And you've used sparkling rubies for the eyes. Perfect!"

"Thank you, Your Majesty," said the Silversmith, delighted Charm was so pleased with her work. "I took the greatest care when casting it. I had only one precious cupful of silver to make it. In fact, I used all but one drop!"

"One drop?" echoed Charm. "Just think! One drop is all we have left of the Silver Pool after *thousands* of years of plenty. I can't believe how thoughtless we've been not to remember Agapogo for her priceless legacy, until now." The queen placed the crown carefully on her head, trying it for size. "It is lovely," she said, "but it can never take the place of my charm bracelet."

"Why, of course not," said the Silversmith. "Nothing will ever take the place of the magical charms. Until they are found, we remain in peril. The crown is merely a token of our respect for Agapogo, after so many years of neglect."

"Will Agapogo be appeased?" asked Charm. "Will she know you sacrificed the last of the silver in her honour?"

"I believe so," said the Silversmith. "Perhaps you could wear the crown on a special occasion?"

Charm thought for a moment.

"I have it!" she announced. "I shall declare a holiday. It will be known as Agapogo Day!"

The Silversmith smiled.

"That is a very good idea, Your Majesty," she said.

Two

Zorgan was pleased with himself. Only the most powerful sorcerer could make Agapogo drain the Silver Pool.

"You checked the pool as I ordered?" Zorgan shot the question at his pixies hovering nearby.

"Yes, Master," said Nix. "We flew right to the bottom. It was very, very hot down there!"

"We couldn't find any silver," confirmed Dina. "Not a drop!"

"Good, good," said Zorgan.

He stood stroking his pet bandrall,✶ Vanda, imagining, with considerable relish, the horrified look that must have crossed the

* * * * * * * * * * * * * *

✶Bandrall – rare flying mammal, native to Karisma

12

Silversmith's face when she'd discovered the empty pool.

A sharp pain in his wrist jolted Zorgan back to reality. He rubbed the scar where once, for a fleeting moment, he had worn the fabulous charm bracelet, the bracelet that could never be his! He was sure the Silversmith had enchanted it, causing it to burn him so cruelly. Well, he'd had his revenge. His thin lips twisted in a sneer.

"Serves her right!" he said. "But now I must attend to a more urgent matter. Sesame Brown!"

The sorcerer knew all about Sesame's last visit to Karisma, the pixies had given him a full report, but he'd been furious with them for allowing Sesame to escape with another charm.

"We must find a way to stop her coming here again," he told Vanda, gently placing her on a perch. "Hm! I have an idea . . ."

Zorgan hurried to the Star Room to consult his crystal ball. In the dim light, the sphere glowed eerily like a moon. Zorgan peered into the shimmering mist, swirling around inside. Would the magic work? Would it be powerful enough to take him far beyond the reaches of Karisma to the

13

Outworld? It was worth a try. There was urgency in his voice as he intoned:

"Take me now through time and space,
That I may see the Seeker's face;
Oh mystic powers reveal to me,
The one I seek is – Sesame!"

Slowly the mist cleared. At first there was nothing. Then, gradually, a picture of blue sky and sea appeared. Seconds went by. Zorgan drummed his fingers impatiently on the glass.

"Come on, come on!" he growled.

The image faded, a small white cottage appeared, wavered and changed to show an odd-shaped room, then suddenly a girl's smiling face swam into view. Zorgan could barely contain his excitement. It must be Sesame. He fixed his cold black eyes on her.

"Vermy* Outworlder!** You'll never come here again, you, you—"

Zorgan controlled himself. The vision wouldn't last for long and there was hardly any time left to cast the spell. Hastily he began to chant:

"Shades and shadows cloud your eyes-" but got no further, before a blinding flash lit up the Star Room.

* *

Vermy – a miserable worm

** Outworlder* – the name Karismans call someone from our world

14

When Zorgan had recovered from the shock, when he looked once more into the crystal ball, Sesame had gone! She had simply vanished into thin air and, try as he might, Zorgan could not bring her back.

Zorgan was livid. The mist refused to clear. It seemed as if another, more powerful force was present – an invisible, protective shield was clouding his vision of Sesame.

"I *will* find a way to stop her," he promised himself. "It is only a matter of time."

Three

"I won't see my favourite pony for two whole weeks!" groaned Sesame. She was talking to her riding instructor, Jodie Luck.

Jodie had found Sesame in the stable, saying goodbye to Silver. It was the start of the summer holidays and Sesame had spent the day helping with the ponies.

"Of course!" said Jodie, remembering something Sesame had mentioned earlier. "You're going away tomorrow aren't you?"

"Yes," said Sesame. "We're going to Cornwall. Lossy and Maddy are coming. I wish you could come too."

Jodie smiled.

"Thank you," she said, touched by Sesame's warmth. "But who would take care of the ponies?"

"Mmm," said Sesame, stroking Silver's nose. "Someone has to look after *you*!"

Silver gave a friendly snort, as if he understood every word.

"Is Lossy your mum?" asked Jodie.

"No, she's my gran," said Sesame. "Mum died when I was a baby."

"Sorry," said Jodie.

"That's OK," said Sesame. "Poppy, that's my mum, died in a car crash. I live with—"

Just then, Nic Brown arrived to take Sesame home.

"Hi Dad!" she said, giving Silver one last hug.

Jodie and Nic had met once before. Jodie remembered his twinkling, nut-brown eyes.

"Hello," she said, blushing. "Sesame was just telling me about—"

At that moment her mobile rang and she fished it out of her pocket.

"Who? Oh, yes. Friday will be fine—"

She broke off to mouth "sorry" to Nic and "have a good time" to Sesame, before continuing.

"Bye," said Nic, wishing he could stay longer.

As they were walking to the car, Sesame couldn't help noticing how happy he looked.

"I think Jodie's great," she remarked, casually.

"Mmm," said Nic. "So do I . . ."

Sesame spotted it first.

"Look!" she cried. "The sea!"

There was a cheer from the others in the car. Nic, Lossy, Sesame and Maddy had been driving down a twisty Cornish lane, flanked by windblown trees and banks of wildflowers. Rounding a corner they saw a

small white cottage perched on a hill. It had a yellow front door and a thatched roof; beyond was a sandy cove and the blue Atlantic Ocean. Nic stopped the car.

"Cliff Cottage, Dad?" queried Sesame, reading the name on the gate.

Nic checked the holiday brochure.

"Yes," he said. "And that's Gullhilly Cove."

"Marvellous!" said Lossy. "Let's go in."

The cottage was very cosy. It had low-beamed ceilings and brightly-coloured rugs on the floors. Upstairs were three lovely bedrooms. When Sesame

   20

discovered the smallest, she called Maddy to come
and see it.

"This is ours!" she said.

It was an odd-shaped room with a latticed window
beneath the eaves and two beds with patchwork quilts.
Maddy came in and dumped her case on the floor.

"Fab!" she said.

Quickly the girls unpacked. Maddy put her things
away neatly in a drawer, Sesame stuffed hers in
anyhow, except for the last item, which she placed
carefully by her bed. It was her jewellery box. Maddy
looked surprised.

"You brought it?" she said.

"Of course," said Sesame, lifting the lid to check that the beautiful silver bracelet and the heart and horseshoe charms were in place. She dropped her voice to a whisper. "If we go to Karisma and find another charm, I'll have to keep it safe, won't I?"

"Right," said Maddy. "You really believe we're going back?"

Sesame hesitated for a moment before answering. She wondered if she *would* find a way to Karisma. Supposing she could *never* go there again! Her tummy did a backwards flip. She felt wobbly. Maddy was looking at her in a funny way.

"What's up, Ses?" she asked.

"N-n-nothing," said Sesame. "I felt a bit strange. But I'm fine now."

"Karisma?" prompted Maddy.

"Yes," said Sesame. "We'll get there somehow!"

She looked inside her jewellery box again before closing the lid.

"Eleven charms are still missing, remember? Sesame Brown will track them down!"

Just then Lossy popped her head round the door.

"Anyone for the beach?" she said.

22

Four

Agapogo was free at last. The Silversmith had broken Zorgan's curse, just in time to save the Silver Pool. Now Agapogo was thirsty for revenge on the wicked magician.

Entering a cavern at the heart of Mount Fortuna, the dragon spectre looked around. Ghostly eyes glowed like red-hot coals and, in a while, Agapogo spotted the mound. There, heaped upon the sandy floor, was a clutch of eggs with purple spots. They were unmistakably drakon✶ eggs!

There are few who would not shudder at the very mention of a drakon. Dragon bugs (as they are commonly known) shoot flames from their jaws and are among the largest, most dangerous insects in

* *

✶ **Drakon** – a large, fire-breathing insect

23

Karisma. Farmers especially fear them, for a drakoon* of fire-breathing drakons can destroy a crop of clover in no time!

Now these particular eggs had been laid a long time ago. The mother had hidden them deep inside the cavern, where she knew they would be safe. It could be years before the temperature was just right for her young to hatch, because drakon eggs require heat – intense heat – and Agapogo knew that too.

"My beauties!" Agapogo whispered tenderly, as if the eggs were her own. "Your time has come!"

Then she took the deepest breath and filled her nostrils with a headwind from the East, a tailwind from the West, a gale from the North and a hurricane from the South. When she was full to bursting she ROARED! And the force of her breath was like a scorching whirlwind. Sparks whizzed round like Catherine wheels, until they were spinning so fast that they turned into a massive ball of fire. Then the fireball blasted its way up through a crack in the mountain and burst out of the top with an ear-splitting

BANG!

* *

Drakoon – collective name for a large number of drakons

It was as if a thousand fireworks had exploded at once!

Meanwhile, the heat in the cavern grew hotter and hotter. When it was as hot as a furnace, the eggs split open.

CRACK!
CRACK! CRACK!

One by one the drakons emerged from their splintered shells. Before long, there was a drakoon of dragon bugs spitting fire and ready to fly!

Agapogo spoke to them in Dracodictum*, the language of dragons, which the drakons understood perfectly.

"Drakons rise, your wings unfold,
The time has come, you must be bold.
To Zorgan's Tower, my fiery friends,
I need your help to make amends.
Yes, haste to where the wizard dwells
And there you'll find his books of spells.
Feast on these and take your fill
To satisfy my vengeful will!"

Dracodictum – the language of dragons

As soon as Agapogo finished speaking, the drakons unfolded their wings, glowing with flaming colours – blue, orange and red. In the next instant, the air was alive with wildly fluttering drakons soaring up through the vent. They poured from the top of Mount Fortuna and, like fiery locusts, swarmed towards Zorgan's Tower.

Five

The first week of the holiday went by in a flash. Every day Sesame and Maddy went swimming or sightseeing with Nic and Lossy; and sometimes the girls went shopping on their own, at the little fishing village nearby.

One day Sesame wore her red top with the sparkly heart and put on her favourite necklace – the locket with pictures of Nic and Poppy inside. As she fastened the clasp Sesame felt a tingle at the nape of her neck and, in that moment, any doubts she'd had about returning to Karisma simply faded away. She didn't know why, but she had a feeling today was going to be special!

After breakfast they all walked down the winding cliff path to Gullhilly Cove. Nic had planned to spend the morning surfing and had brought his board.

"Should catch some good ones today," he said, scrutinising the waves. "See you later!"

"Bye, Dad. Don't fall off!" Sesame called after him, as he went to join a group of surfers. Then she turned to Maddy. "Come on. Let's explore."

"Have fun," said Lossy, settling down to read her book. "But stay where I can see you."

"We will," the girls promised, as they ran off across the beach. For a while they were absorbed peering into rock pools, finding tiny crabs, starfish and pretty pebbles as they wandered further and further along the beach.

"Maybe we should go back now?" suggested Maddy, looking around anxiously for Sesame's gran. Lossy was nowhere in sight, but she saw Nic, splashing around in the surf. "Oh! Your dad's just fallen off his board!"

Sesame goggled her eyes.

"Trust Dad," she said.

She was about to follow Maddy, when she came across a cave at the foot of the cliff.

29

"Wait!" she cried. "I'm going to have a look in here."

Maddy scrambled over the rocks after her.

"Ooo," she said, peering into the gloomy cavern. "It's really spooky!"

Her voice echoed round the walls and came ringing back, to mock her.

SPOOOKY OOOKYOOOKY!

"It's OK," said Sesame, walking in boldly. Almost immediately her eye caught something bright, sparkling above her head and, glancing up, she gave a gasp of surprise. "Maddy! Come here. This is amazing."

"What is?" said Maddy, taking a few hesitant paces inside. She felt cold and afraid.

"Look at these shells," said Sesame. "There must be hundreds of them!"

And so there were. The roof of the cave was studded with glistening, silvery fossils, shimmering with a translucent light of their own. For a second or two, Sesame and Maddy stood gazing at them. Then, almost without thinking, they started walking along the narrow passageway, following the luminous trail of shells, until Sesame stopped dead in her tracks.

"Wh-what?" whispered Maddy.

"There," said Sesame, pointing to a spot ahead of them. "A red light. Waving about. See?"

Maddy looked over Sesame's shoulder and froze. She was convinced it was a terrible, red-eyed monster.

"I'm really scared, Ses. Let's go."

But Sesame took her by the arm. She felt drawn towards the flickering light and walked slowly forward.

"Stay close to me," she told Maddy. "It'll be all right. I've got the weirdest feeling—"

She broke off because the rippling light suddenly burst into a shower of silvery stars.

"Wow!" cried the girls together.

And next thing they knew they were floating, tumbling, falling through a thousand twinkling stars into another world . . .

Six

Boom!

Zorgan was in his Star Room when he heard the thud of an explosion. The air shook. The tower shuddered.

"Quisto!"* he exclaimed. "What was that?"

The pixies, Nix and Dina, heard it too. Sensing their master was in danger, they immediately flew to his side. Vanda flew round in circles, screeching.

In the distance Zorgan saw smoke billowing from Mount Fortuna.

"Extraordinary," he murmured, half-fascinated, half-fearful of this unusual happening. Mount Fortuna had never erupted before. Why now?

Nix and Dina surveyed the scene.

"Look, Master," said Nix, pointing to a dark, sinister-looking cloud, silhouetted against the sky.

The magician narrowed his eyes, scanning the horizon.

"Debris" concluded Zorgan. "Smuts from the smoke."

* *

*Quisto – an exclamation of surprise

"No, Master," said Nix, setting her eyeball lenses to 'zoom'. Her cold, crystal eyes glinted with excitement. "Bugs!"

"Spitting fire!" added Dina.

Zorgan looked again. The cloud was heading towards them fast, countless flaming lights moving and weaving as one.

"Identify!" he barked.

"Drakons!" chorused the pixies.

"Shut the tower!" yelled Zorgan. "We're under attack!"

Nix and Dina raced around the tower slamming windows and doors. But the speed of the advancing drakons took them all by surprise. A cluster came hurtling against a window –

CRASH!

– smashing the glass into a thousand pieces. Within seconds the Star Room was alive with fire-spewing bugs. Flasks and test tubes shattered in their fiery breath and foul-smelling potions spilled on the floor.

Zorgan uttered the first insect-zapping curse he could think of.

"STUPIFLY!" he cried, pointing his wand at a passing drakon. But the curse missed the bug, backfired and singed his beard.

33

Meanwhile Nix and Dina were fiercely fighting with bug swats, batting and swishing drakons. But still they kept coming.

Zorgan realised with horror that they were making for his library; his magnificent collection of leather-bound volumes, prized copies of chants and incantations, books of spells, ancient myths and magic.

"Stop them!" he ordered the pixies. "Save my books!"

Nix and Dina armed themselves with foam pistols.

SWOOOSH!

WHOOOSH!

They met the oncoming drakons with powerful blasts of foaming froth, which sent some bugs spiralling and fizzling to the ground. But most of them

ducked and dived their way through to the
library, setting the bookshelves ablaze.

When Zorgan saw the pixies had
failed, he was furious. He must do
something! Fighting his way through the fire, he
managed to rescue a volume of **Advanced Weather
Spells** by Windy Doldrums, only slightly singed
round the edges. He flipped the pages and, finding a
useful rain spell, rapidly chanted the words.

After a deafening clap of
thunder and a streak of lightning,
came the rain. It poured in torrents
through the open windows and eventually put out
the flames. All around lay Zorgan's precious
books, their pages charred and rain-soaked.

Then an odd thing happened. Letters and
words began to float off the pages. Spells,
curses and incantations — indeed the very words
Zorgan had chanted to invoke the spirit of Agapogo
— were now jumbled up and spiralling about the
room. Worse still, the drakons were eating them!

At last, when they had eaten their fill, the bugs flew away leaving Zorgan in the ruins of his once beautiful library.

"This is Agapogo's doing!" he shouted. "She sent those balam* bugs here. I'll get my own back, you'll see. Now, you useless pixies, clear up this mess!"

* *
*Balam – cursed, an angry exclamation

Seven

Sesame and Maddy tumbled through the air like clothes in a washing machine. Suddenly, they dropped straight down and landed on a pile of feathers. Unfortunately, the feathers belonged to Feenix the firebird, who shot into the air with a terrified SQUAWK!

Sesame and Maddy went sprawling.

"Flaming Fizzwigs!" cried Feenix. "Mind where you plonk yourselves!"

The girls stood up. An enormous bird with magnificent red and gold plummage was glaring at them. She looked most annoyed.

"Sorry," said Sesame, brushing a feather off her nose. "We didn't *mean* to land on you."

"Couldn't help it," added Maddy.

Feenix eyed them inquisitively, uttering "Ah!" and "Hm!" every now and again. Then something must have clicked, because suddenly she greeted them enthusiastically.

"Sesame Brown? Maddy Webb? Charmseekers from the Outworld?"* she asked.

"Right," replied Sesame.

"That's us," said Maddy.

"Oh, my!" said Feenix. "I've heard all about you Charmseekers. And here you are at my gate. I'm Feenix. Gatekeeper Three. Welcome to Karisma!"

Sesame and Maddy looked at each other. They felt as famous as pop stars! Looking around they saw they were standing by a wrought-iron gate set in a wall and, through the ironwork, they could make out a street.

"Where are we?" asked Sesame.

"Lantern Hill," replied Feenix. "There's a carnival here today. It's Agapogo Day."

★ AGAPOGO DAY ★
Her Majesty Queen Charm has proclaimed that today shall be a holiday, to be celebrated throughout Karisma, in honour of Agapogo, the Dragon of the Silver Pool.
By Royal Command

★

* *

*Outworld — the name Karismans call our world

"Sounds fun!" said Sesame. "But we're here to look for the missing charms."

"How long have we got?" asked Maddy.

"Be back before the bell strikes three," warned Feenix.

"Come on, Maddy," said Sesame. "Let's go."

The two set off down a narrow street hung with lanterns and paper dragons. The air felt chilly as they walked along and when some warmly-dressed Karismans gave them quizzical looks, Sesame and Maddy realised they were still dressed for the beach.

"We must look totally bonkers!" said Sesame. "It's winter here."

"I've got goose-bumps," complained Maddy, vigorously rubbing her arms.

Turning a corner at the end of the street, they came to a busy market. It was full of gaily decorated carts and stalls with traders shouting their wares. Soon Sesame and Maddy found themselves being jostled along past rows of stallholders selling dragon cakes, masks, lanterns and lollipops. And everywhere people were enjoying themselves and getting ready for the carnival that night.

"This is crazy," said Maddy, squeezing past a hairy

troll selling firecrackers. "We won't find any charms here. Let's try somewhere else."

"OK," agreed Sesame. "Lead the way!"

She was about to follow Maddy through the market, when

CRICK-CRACK! WEEEEEEEEEEEEE!

A fizzing firecracker shot past her. The hairy troll had set one off for fun! Sesame saw the firework land by a girl selling pots and potions from a tray. Before Sesame could shout a warning –

BANG! The cracker went off in a shower of sparks. The startled girl tipped up her tray and everything fell at her feet.

"Doofer!"* she yelled at the troll, who seemed to think it was very funny. "I hate trolls!" She burst into tears.

Straightaway Sesame went to comfort her.

"Don't cry," she said. "I'll help you."

Together they gathered up all the bottles, pots and jars. The girl was dressed in green and Sesame noticed she had a pair of wings folded neatly down her back. She was a fairy!  When she saw Sesame looking at her, she smiled.

"I'm Quilla," she said. "And you're the Seeker from the Outworld, aren't you?"

"Yes," said Sesame, quite surprised. "Sesame Brown. And this is my friend—"

She stopped, remembering she should have been following Maddy. Sesame looked around but Maddy was nowhere in sight.

"I must go, Quilla," she said, urgently.

* *

* **Doofer** – idiot of the first order, brainless

41

"Here, take this," said Quilla, handing her a pot.

"What is it?" asked Sesame.

"Vanishing Cream," said Quilla. "To thank you for helping me. Works like magic. You may need it sooner than you think! Setfair, ✷ Seeker."

"Thanks!" said Sesame, wondering what she meant. But she was worried about Maddy, so putting the pot in her pocket, she hurried away.

Meanwhile Maddy was waiting anxiously near the market. She was sure Sesame had been right behind her. She was about to look for her when a woman

✷ Setfair — goodbye and good luck

42

with wild, black hair grabbed her shoulder. Most of her face was hidden behind a mask. All Maddy saw were bright red lips, curled in an icy smile.

"Waiting for someone?" enquired the woman sweetly. But there was a chilling edge to her tone.

"Er . . . yes," said Maddy.

The woman took a step closer.

"Who? I may be able to help?"

"My-my friend, Ses-sesame," stammered Maddy, desperately wishing Ses would appear.

"Sssssssesameee!" hissed the woman, like a snake spitting venom. "Well, why don't we look for *Sesame* together!"

It was not a question. The woman had Maddy's arm in a vice-like grip.

"Come along—"

"No!" cried Maddy, wrenching herself free as she caught sight of Sesame.

"Ses! Ses! I'm here!" she yelled.

Sesame could see she looked upset.

"I'm really sorry," she said. "I stopped to—"

But Maddy wasn't listening.

"Did you see her?" she said.

"Who?" asked Sesame.

"That woman in a mask!" said Maddy, pointing.

But when they looked, the woman was nowhere to be seen. Maddy quickly told Sesame what had happened.

"I wonder if it was Morbrecia?" said Sesame, grimly. "She knows we're after the charms. Remember last time we were here? She was going to throw us to the skreels!"*

"You're right!" said Maddy.

"We'll stick together from now on," said Sesame. "The sooner we find another charm the better."

As they started up Lantern Hill, they heard the bell strike one.

They followed the road past houses with roofs of brightly coloured glass, which sparkled like jewels in the bright, wintry sun. Everywhere there were happy Karismans enjoying the new holiday Queen Charm had decreed. But neither of them noticed the shadowy figure of Morbrecia prowling after them.

As they climbed the hill, Sesame told Maddy about

* *

* Skreel – small flesh-eating fish

her meeting with the fairy, Quilla. In a while, they came to the entrance of a park and ahead lay several pathways.

"Which path?" said Maddy.

"That one," said Sesame, choosing a path that wound between trees, strung with lanterns. As they went, they kept a sharp look-out for charms.

"I've forgotten which ones are missing," said Maddy, peering under a bush.

Sesame knew them all by heart and reeled them off easily.

"There's a key, coin, cat and clover," she began. "Moon, lantern, star – that's seven – a dolphin, butterfly, shell and snowflake."

Maddy moaned.

"They could be anywhere," she said.

"We'll find them," said Sesame, confidently. "Sesame Brown will track them down!"

They carried on up the hill and when they were near the top, Sesame felt a tingle at the back of her neck. She felt her locket. Yes! There it was again. Sesame looked around and saw the crest of the hill was covered with enormous crystalline rocks, speckled pink and white. Some balanced precariously, one on top of the other; some lay tilting crazily, as if a giant had flung them there in a tantrum.

A twinkling light caught Sesame's eye. The biggest rock was topped with a lantern; the light inside was

45

flashing and, in her imagination, Sesame thought the beacon was sending her a signal.

"Let's try up there," she said to Maddy. "We might be lucky."

They clambered over boulders, smoothed by wind and weather. It wasn't easy; there were only a few craggy places to hold, but, at last, they reached the beacon. They were walking round it when, all of a sudden, Maddy tripped.

"Ooops!" she cried, falling flat on her face.

"You OK?" said Sesame, helping her up.

"Yeah," said Maddy. "I must've—"

Sesame was already pointing to something, half-buried in the ground.

"You fell over this," she said, scraping away some dirt. She revealed a block of stone.

"It looks like a step," said Maddy.

Then Sesame spotted more steps, leading to a yawning hole in the rock.

"There's a cave!" she exclaimed.

Maddy groaned, remembering the one they'd found in Cornwall.

"No more caves, Ses!" she said. "Anyway, I'm cold enough already. I bet it's freezing in there."

"Come on," pleaded Sesame. "Just a quick look? Promise." And she gave Maddy their secret hand sign.

= True. I'll keep my word!

46

Reluctantly, Maddy followed Sesame inside. As she did, she thought she heard soft footfalls behind her. But when she turned to look, there was nothing there.

To Sesame and Maddy's surprise, the cave felt strangely warm. A pinkish light pulsed – bright then dim – as if the cave itself was transmitting a glow. Sesame went ahead, searching and searching for a charm she was sure they would find. The further they went, the warmer it became. Suddenly, Maddy felt a blast of hot air above her head and gave a startled shout.

"What's up?" said Sesame, wheeling round.

"The-there," stammered Maddy, pointing to a ledge.

They were looking at a mass of fierce-looking bugs, every one of them breathing fire! By chance, the girls had disturbed some drakons, who had settled there after their attack on Zorgan.

Sesame gulped.

"They don't seem pleased to see us," she quipped.

Maddy backed away.

"Time to go, Ses," she said. "Like, now!"

"R-i-g-h-t," said Sesame, her eyes fixed on the terrifying insects. The bugs were getting madder by the minute, flapping their wings and spitting fire. Slowly she began to edge towards Maddy then stopped suddenly.

She'd spotted something small and silver, glistening on the ledge.

"Maddy, wait!" she hissed. "There's something up there. See? Next to that big bug?"

"No! I'm not looking," said Maddy, her voice trembling with fear. "I don't care what it is. Come on, Ses. We've got to get out of here!"

But Sesame ignored her friend. She stood on tip-toe and stretched out her arm to reach the ledge. The nearest drakon thought she was going to attack and aimed a fiery jet at her.

"Ouch!" yelled Sesame, snatching back her hand to blow on her sore fingers. Flattening herself against the wall she tried again, feeling along the ledge until, at last, her fingers closed around a small, metal object. Clasping it tightly, she and Maddy ran from the cave.

"Phew!" said Maddy. "Those bugs were the scariest!"

"I know," Sesame said, opening her palm. "But it was worth it. Look. I've found another charm!"

"The shell!" Maddy gasped, her eyes wide with delight. "Well done, Ses."

Sesame held up the precious little charm. The sun was setting and the girls watched it glisten in the evening glow. It was beautiful.

But even as they stood there, a shadow fell across their path. Sesame and Maddy squealed with fright. It was the woman in the mask.

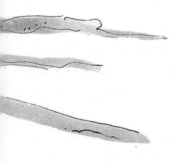

Eight

It all happened so quickly.
One moment Sesame was holding
the shell and the next, she wasn't. Morbrecia's
skinny arm shot out and snatched the charm
from her hand.

"Thank you!" said Morbrecia, sarcastically. "This
is mine. Mine, d'you hear? Every one of the charms
belongs to ME!"

"No!" cried Sesame, struggling to her feet.

"Vermy Outworlder!" snarled Morbrecia. "You
dare to challenge me? *Princess* Morbrecia! Out of my
way!" And she pushed Sesame back with her boot.

"Give it back!" cried Maddy fiercely, and made a
grab for Morbrecia's ankle. But she was too late.
Morbrecia stepped nimbly aside and made off with
the charm.

"After her!" yelled Sesame.

And they ran as they'd never run before. But
Morbrecia ran even faster – scarily fast – her long
black hair streaming in the wind. And before they
knew it, they were out of the park and pelting down
the road after the fleeing princess.

"We'll never catch her," panted Maddy.

"Come on," said Sesame. "We can't let her get away. We must get the charm back."

But as Morbrecia raced on her way, a child pulling

a toy dragon ran in front of her . . .

"Blatz!"* cried Morbrecia, as she went head-over-heels. "Ugh!" she groaned, as she landed in an enormous puddle. "AAAAARH!" she screamed, as the charm flew out of her hand and rolled, just out of reach.

Sesame saw her chance and dived for the charm.

"Got it!" she cried, her heart thumping. She clasped the shell tightly in her fist and put it in her pocket.

"Wicked!" said Maddy, giggling at Morbrecia in the puddle.

"Oh, help!" cried Sesame. "Morbrecia's up again. Run!"

 And the bell struck two.

* *

*Blatz – a really angry exclamation

54

A merry carnival procession was wending its way through the town. Sesame and Maddy dodged in and out of floats, fire-eaters and torch-bearers in their efforts to escape from Morbrecia. She looked mad with rage as she chased after them.

As a magnificent horse-drawn carriage came along, the Charmseekers had to leap aside. It was carrying none other than Queen Charm! She was proudly wearing the Crown of Agapogo and waving to the crowds.

For a split-second, Sesame thought the queen looked straight at her! Could she sense the power of the charm so near? Next thing she knew, Maddy was tugging at her arm.

"Look," she said, pointing to a spectacular dragon train. "Let's hide."

"Good idea," said Sesame.

The girls slipped under the scaly canopy and joined the line of Karisman children, who were supporting the dragon train above their heads.

"Quisto!" exclaimed a very surprised Karisman boy, running in the line.

"Don't mind us," said Maddy. "Just pretend we're not here—"

And Sesame suddenly remembered the Vanishing Cream. *"You may need this sooner than you think!"* Quilla had told her. Well, she needed it right now!

Nine

"Will it hurt?" whispered Maddy, nervously. "Quilla didn't say," said Sesame, keeping her voice low. "We'll just have to put it on and see."

The dragon train had come to an abrupt halt and Sesame had just told Maddy about the Vanishing Cream. Morbrecia was close and cursing. It was only a matter of seconds before she discovered them. They had to act fast. Sesame opened the pot.

"Me first," said Maddy, bravely.

"Oh, Maddy!" whispered Sesame. "Supposing we never see each other again? You're my best friend!"

"And you're mine," said Maddy, giving Sesame a hug. "The bestest ever! But we've got to get away from Morbrecia, right?"

Sesame nodded. She held out the pot and watched anxiously as Maddy put a blob of bright blue cream on her finger.

"Here goes!" she said, rubbing it into her cheeks. She felt a bit wobbly, then *Ping!*

"Did it work?" said Maddy's voice nearby.

"Um . . . almost," said Sesame. "I can still see your feet."

"Oh, no!" wailed Maddy. "I didn't put enough—"
She stopped.

"Ses!" she cried. "Morbrecia's behind you!"

Morbrecia made a lunge for Sesame. But Sesame ducked, slapped on the cream and *Pop!* She disappeared before Morbrecia's eyes.

Leaping out of the dragon, the two almost invisible Charmseekers had to find their way back to the gate. They wove their way through a milling crowd of revellers and carnival floats. Maddy swerved round a stilt-walker to avoid a nasty collision; Sesame tripped over an excited dog, which barked furiously at its invisible assailant. But when they paused to catch their breath, they noticed with horror that the Vanishing Cream was wearing off and Morbrecia was not far behind. She screeched with glee when she caught sight of the Charmseekers again.

"Come on," gasped Sesame. "There's Feenix. One last sprint and we're there."

Morbrecia was after them, in full cry, and above her curses they heard the bell CLANG.

"Hurry! Hurry!" cried Feenix, fluttering up and down. The bell clanged twice. "One more strike and the gate shuts!"

As the bell struck three, the Charmseekers threw themselves through the closing gate. Morbrecia flung herself at Sesame but she was too late.
All Sesame left behind was a shoe.

Spotted on Lantern Hill!

Can you spot 10 things the Charmseekers saw?

☆

Spotted paper lantern

Firecracker

Pot of vanishing cream

Bell

Drakon

Shell

Toy dragon with one wing

Crown of Agapogo

Sesame's lost shoe

Morbrecia's mask

☆

☆   ☆

☆

☆

"I got dumped!" said a cheerful voice. "Nearly lost the board. Fantastic wave. Did you see?"

Sesame and Maddy looked up and saw Nic grinning at them.

"Er, I did, Mr Brown," said Maddy, in a daze. She sat up and brushed sand from her knees.

"Mmm," murmured Sesame vaguely, and scrambled to her feet. "Bad luck, Dad."

Little did he know that they'd just been dumped too! Sesame wasn't sure how they'd got back to the beach, but here they were.

Later, when they were alone in their room at Cliff Cottage, Sesame opened her jewellery box. She took the tiny silver shell from her pocket. But before she put it away, they sat for a while looking at it.

"It's so pretty," said Maddy, admiring the way the charm seemed to shimmer with a light of its own. "No wonder Morbrecia was so keen to have it."

Sesame remembered the awful moment Morbrecia had snatched it from her.

"She's scary," she said.

Maddy shivered at the thought of her.

"I bet she's hopping mad we got away," she said.

"Hey! I'm the one hopping around here," said Sesame, wiggling her toes. "Morbrecia grabbed my flip-flop, remember? Gran gave me a really funny look when I said I didn't know how I'd lost it. She knows when I'm fibbing!"

"Isn't it time you told her?" said Maddy. "About Karisma? Everything?"

"I can't, not yet," said Sesame. "She'd only worry or think I was sickening for something. And Dad would think I was making it up."

Maddy nodded. She understood how crazy their adventures would sound. Who would believe them? Sesame placed the little shell in her jewellery box. It gave them both a sense of wonder and achievement to see it now, lying with the bracelet and the heart and horseshoe charms. They were as real as real could be.

"It's our special secret, Maddy," she said. "We're Charmseekers! We must find all the charms, no matter who tries to stop us. I won't give up 'til I've found every one and returned them to Queen Charm."

Sesame snapped the lid shut.

"I can't wait to go back!" she said.

Ten

"Agapogo Day was a great success, Your Majesty," said the Silversmith. "The fireworks on Lantern Hill were spectacular. Fit for a dragon!"

"Yes," said Charm, taking off the Crown of Agapogo and placing it on a velvet cushion. "I shall wear this every year on Agapogo Day. From now on Agapogo will always be remembered for giving us the—"

She broke off. The last time she'd seen the Silversmith only one drop of silver remained of the Silver Pool.

The Silversmith smiled, her eyes twinkling.

"All is well," she said, softly. "Zorgan's wretched curse was broken. I took the last drop of silver and cast it into the magic pool. It will take time, but the magic pool will be restored. If we are careful, we shall have sufficient silver for all our needs."

"Spallah!"✶ exclaimed Charm. "There's only one thing that could please me more. Do you have any news of my charms?"

* *

✶ Spallah – excellent, a triumphant expression

"Indeed I do," said the Silversmith. "One was found this very day! I believe our Charmseeker, Sesame, has it safely in the Outworld."

Charm clapped her hands with delight. "That is marvellous!" she exclaimed.

"Sesame and her friend were at Lantern Hill," said the Silversmith. "Feenix the gatekeeper was boasting about the Charmseekers coming through her gate. Apparently they had a narrow escape—"

The Silversmith bit her tongue. She hadn't meant to let that slip!

"Escape?" said Charm, sounding concerned. "Were the Charmseekers in danger?"

"Probably gossip . . ." began the Silversmith. But Charm was looking at her so intently, she found herself telling the queen everything she knew. Some Karismans had recognised Morbrecia chasing two Outworlders through Lantern Hill that day. Charm listened but with every word her heart grew heavier.

"My sister . . ." she said, quietly. "Can this be true? Is Morbrecia after the charms?"

"It seems so, Your Majesty," said the Silversmith.

Now Charm knew what the Silversmith had feared all along.

"So Morbrecia stole my bracelet!" she said. Her eyes opened wide with horror as she recalled that terrible night. "My sister was the SPIDER!"

Alone in her workshop once more, the Silversmith reflects on all that has happened. Of the thirteen magic candles, one more has flickered and gone out. It is the candle that bears the name of the little shell. Now ten candles glow and each will burn brightly until its missing charm is found. She knows Sesame will return soon. She has chosen well. Sesame won't give up, until her quest is over.

But she fears for her special Charmseeker. Zorgan will do his best to thwart Sesame's mission and Morbrecia will stop at nothing to recover the charms. Oh! There is such bitterness in Morbrecia's heart, such jealousy of her sister, Charm.

But that is another story. It must be told another day!

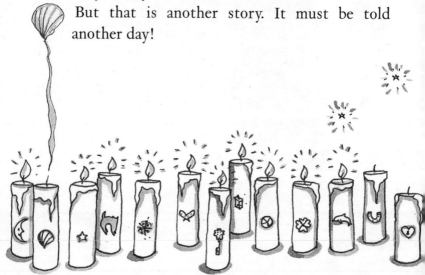

Acknowledgments

I owe a debt of gratitude to all those who have worked behind the scenes at Orion Children's Books and beyond to bring the *Charmseekers* books and their thirteen delightful charms to you. Since it would take more space than this edition allows to mention individuals by name, suffice it to say that I'm hugely grateful to my publishers and everyone involved with the publication of this series. In particular, my special thanks go to: my publisher, Fiona Kennedy, for her faith in believing I could write way beyond my own expectations. Her creative, tactful and skilful editing kept Sesame Brown on the right track and helped me to write a better story; my agent, Rosemary Sandberg; Jenny Glencross and Jane Hughes (Editorial); Alex Nicholas and Helen Speedy (Rights) Loulou Clark and Helen Ewing (Design); Clare Hennessy (Production); Jessica Killingley and Jo Dawson (Marketing); Pandora White (Orion Audio Books); Imogen Adams (Website designer – www.hammerinheels.com); Neil Pymer, the *real* Spinner Shindigs, for kind permission to use his name; and last, but by no means least, a million thanks go to my husband Tom for his inexhaustible patience, critical appraisal and support along the way.

Georgie Adams